The Devil's Spectacles

By

Wilkie Collins

British Library Cataloguing-in-Publication Data
A catalogue record for this book is available from the
British Library

Contents

Wilkie Collins

William Wilkie Collins was born in Marylebone, London in 1824. His family enrolled him at the Maida Hill Academy in 1835, but then took him to France and Italy with them between 1836 and 1838. Collins later recalled that in Italy he learned more "which has been of use to me, among the scenery, the pictures, and the people, than I ever learned at school." Returning to England, Collins attended Cole's boarding school, and completed his education in 1841, after which he was apprenticed to the tea merchants Antrobus & Co. in the Strand.

In 1846, Collins became a law student at Lincoln's Inn, and was called to the bar in 1851, although he never practiced. It was in 1848, a year after the death of his father, that he published his first book, The Memoirs of the Life of William Collins, Esq., R.A., to good reviews. This was followed by an historical novel, Antonina (1850) and three contemporary novels, Basil (1852), Hide and Seek (1854) and The Dead Secret (1857). During the 1850s, however, Collins' main source of income came through journalism. Primarily, he wrote for Household Words, a publication owned and ran by Charles Dickens, with whom Collins had a close friendship. It was also during this decade that Collins began to take large amounts of opium to combat 'rheumatic gout', a form of arthritis he suffered from.

The 1860s saw Collins' creative high-point, and it was during this decade that he achieved fame and critical acclaim, with his four major novels, The Woman in White (1860), No Name (1862), Armadale (1866) and The Moonstone (1868). These were all hugely popular; The Woman in White, for example, ran to seven editions in the first year of publication, and is now regarded as the archetypal sensation novel. The Moonstone, meanwhile is seen by many as the first true detective novel – T. S. Eliot called it "the first, the longest, and the best of modern English detective novels...in a genre invented by Collins and not by Poe."

During the last two decades of his life, Collins' popularity waned. This was due in part to the death of Dickens, and in part to his increasing dependence on opium. It also had a lot to do with his stylistic shift away from the sensational thrillers that his made his name onto works more centred on social commentary; Jezebel's Daughter (1880), for example, advocated humane treatment of lunatics, whilst Heart and Science (1883) condemned vivisection. During the 1880s, Collins' health declined rapidly. In June of 1889, Collins suffered a stroke, and died as a result of further complications three months later, aged 65.

I. MEMOIRS OF AN ARCTIC VOYAGER

He says, sir, he thinks he's nigh to his latter end, and he would like, if convenient, to see you before he goes.'

'Do you mean before he dies?'

'That's about it, sir.'

I was in no humour (for reasons to be hereafter mentioned) for seeing anybody, under disastrous circumstances of any sort; but the person who had sent me word that he was 'nigh to his latter end' had special claims on my consideration.

He was an old sailor, who had first seen blue water under the protection of my father, then a post-captain in the navy. Born on our estate, and the only male survivor of our head gamekeeper's family of seven children, he had received a good education through my father's kindness, and he ought to have got on well in the world; but he was one of those born vagabonds who set education at defiance. His term of service having expired, he disappeared for many years. During part of the time he was supposed to have been employed in the merchant navy. At the end of that long interval he turned up one day at our country house, an invalided man, without a penny in his pocket. My good father, then nearing the end of his life, was invalided too. Whether he had a fellow-feeling for the helpless creature whom he had once befriended, or whether he only took counsel of his own generous nature, it is now needless to inquire. He appointed Septimus Notman to be lodge-keeper at the second of our two park gates, and he recommended Septimus to my personal care on his deathbed. 'I'm afraid he's an old scoundrel,' my father confessed; 'but somebody must look after him as long as he lasts, and if you don't take his part, Alfred, nobody else will.' After this Septimus kept his place at the gate while we were in the country. When we returned to our London house the second gate was closed. The old sailor was lodged (by a strong exertion of my influence) in a room over a disused stable, which our coachman had proposed to turn into a hayloft. Everybody disliked Septimus Notman. He was said to be mad; to be a liar, a hypocrite, a vicious wretch, and a disagreeable brute. There were people who even reported that he had been a pirate during the time when we lost sight of him and who declared, when they were asked for their proof, that his crimes were written in his face. He was not in the least affected by the opinions of his neighbours; he chewed his tobacco and drank his grog, and, in the words of the old song, 'He cared for nobody, no, not he!' Well had my poor father said, that I didn't take his part nobody else would. And shall I tell you a secret? Though I strictly carried out my father's wishes, and though Septimus was disposed in his own rough way to be grateful to me, I didn't like him either.

So I went to the room over the stables (we were in London at the time) with dry eyes and I sat down by his bed and cut up a cake of tobacco for him, and said, 'Well, what's the matter?' as coolly as if he had sent me word that he thought he had caught a cold in the head. 'I'm called away.' Septimus answered, 'and before I go I've got a confession to make, and something useful to offer you. It's reported among the servants, Mr Alfred, that you're in trouble just now between two ladies. You may see your way clear in that matter, sir, if death spares me long enough to say a few last words.'

'Never mind me, Septimus. Has a doctor seen you?'

'The doctor knows no more about me than I know myself. The doctor be --!'

'Have you any last wishes I can attend to?'

'None, sir.'

'Shall I send for a clergyman?'

Septimus Notman looked at me as directly as he could -- he was afflicted with a terrible squint. Otherwise he was a fine, stoutly-built man, with a ruddy face profusely encircled by white hair and whiskers, a hoarse, heavy voice, and the biggest hands I ever saw. He put one of these enormous hands under his pillow before he answered me.

'If you think,' he said, 'that a clergyman will come to a man who has got the Devil's Spectacles here, under his pillow, and who has only to put those Spectacles on to see through that clergyman's clothes, flesh, and what not, and read everything that's written in his secret mind as plain as print, fetch him, Master Alfred -- fetch him!'

I thought the clergyman might not like this, and withdrew my suggestion accordingly. The least I could do, as a matter of common politeness, after giving up the clergyman, was to ask if I might look at the Devil's Spectacles.

'Hear how I came by them first!' said Septimus.

'Will it take long?' I inquired.

9

'It will take long, and it will make your flesh creep.'

I remembered my promise to my father, and placed myself and my flesh at the mercy of Septimus Notman. But he was not ready to begin yet.

'Do you see that white jug?' he said, pointing to the wash-stand.

'Yes. Do you want water?'

'I want grog. There's grog in the white jug. And there's a pewter mug on the chimney-piece. I must be strung up, Master Alfred -- I must be strung up.'

The white jug contained at least half a gallon of rum and water, roughly calculated. I strung him up. In the case of any other dying person I might have hesitated. But a man who possessed the Devil's Spectacles was surely an exception to ordinary rules, and might finish his career and finish his grog at one and the same time.

'Now I'm ready,' he said, 'What do you think I was up to in the time when you all lost sight of me? The latter part of that time, I mean?'

'They say you were a pirate,' I replied.

'Worse than that. Guess again.'

I tried to persuade myself that there might be such a human anomaly as a merciful pirate, and guessed once more.

'A murderer,' I suggested.

'Worse than that. Guess again.'

I declined to guess again. 'Tell me yourself what you have been,' I said.

He answered without the least appearance of

discomposure, 'I've been a Cannibal.'

Perhaps it was weak of me -- but I did certainly start to my feet and make for the door.

'Hear the circumstances,' said Septimus. 'You know the proverb, sir? Circumstances alter cases.'

There was no disputing the proverb. I sat down again. I was a young and tender man, which, in my present position, was certainly against me. But I had very little flesh on my bones and that was in my favour.

'It happened when I went out with the Arctic expedition,' Septimus proceeded. 'I've forgotten all my learning, and lost my memory for dates. The year escapes me, and the latitude and longitude escape me. But I can tell you the rest of it. We were an exploring party, you must know, with sledges. It was getting close to the end of the summer months in those parts, and we were higher than any of them have ever got since to the North Pole. We should have found our way there -- don't you doubt it -- but for three of our best men who fell sick of the scurvy. The second lieutenant, who was in command, called a halt, as the soldiers say. "With this loss of strength," says he, "it's my duty to take you back to the ships. We must let the North Pole be, and pray God that we may have no more invalided men to carry. I give you half an hour's rest before we turn back." The carpenter was one of our sound men. He spoke next. He reported one of the two sledges not fit for service. "How long will you be making it fit?" says the lieutenant. "In a decent climate," says the carpenter, " I should say two or three hours, sir. Here, double that time, at least." You may say why not do without the sledge? I'll tell you why. On account of the sick men to be carried. "Be as quick about it as you can," says the lieutenant: "time means life in our predicament." Most of the men were glad enough to rest. Only two of us murmured at not going on. One was a boatswain's mate; t'other was me. "Do you think the North Pole's the other side of that rising ground there?" says the lieutenant. The boatswain's mate was young and self-conceited. "I should like to try, sir," he says, "if any other man has pluck enough to go along with me." He looked at me when he said that. I wasn't going to have my courage called in question publicly by a slip of a lad; and, moreover, I had a fancy to try for the North Pole, too. I volunteered to go along with him. Our notion, you will understand, was to take a compass and some grub with us; to try what we could find in a couple hours' march forward; and to get back in good time for our duty on the return journey. The lieutenant wouldn't hear of it. "I'm responsible for every man in my charge," says he. "You're a couple of fools. Stay where you are." We were a couple of fools. We watched our opportunity, while they were all unloading the broken-down sledge; and slipped off to try our luck, and get the reward for discovering the North Pole.'

There he stopped, and pointed to the grog. 'Dry-work, talking,' he said. 'Give us a drop more.'

I filled the pewter mug again. And again Septimus Notman emptied it.

'We set our course northwest by north,' he went on; 'and after a while (seeing the ground favoured us) we altered it again to due north. I can't tell you how long we walked (we neither of us had watches) -- but this I'll swear to. Just as the last of the daylight was dying out, we got to the top of a hillock; and there we saw the glimmer of the open Polar Sea! No! not the Sound that enters Kennedy's Channel, which has been mistaken for it, I know -- but the real thing, the still and lonesome Polar Sea! What would you have done in our place? I'll tell you what we did. We sat down on some nice dry snow, and took out our biscuits and grog. Freezing work, do you say? You'll find it in the books, if you don't believe me -- the further north you get in those parts, the less cold there is, and the more open water you find. Ask Captain M'Clure what sort of a bed he slept upon, on the night of October thirtieth, 'fifty-one. Well, and what do you think we did when we had eaten and drunk? Lit our pipes. And what next? Fell fast asleep, after our long walk, on our nice dry snow. And what sort of prospect met us when we woke? Darkness and drizzle and mist. I had the compass, and I tried to set our course on the way back. I could no more see the compass than if I had been blind. We had no means of striking a light, except my match-box. I had left it on the snow by my side when I fell asleep. Not a match would light. As for help of any sort, it was not to be thought of. We couldn't have been less than five miles distant from the place where we had left our messmates. So there we were, the boatswain's mate and me, alone in the desert, lost at the North Pole.'

I began to feel interested. 'You tried to get back, I suppose,

13

dark as it was?' I said.

'We walked till we dropped,' Septimus answered; 'and then we yelled and shouted till we had no voices left; and then we hollowed out a hole in the snow, and waited for daylight.'

'What did you expect when daylight came?'

'I expected nothing, Master Alfred. The boatswain's mate (beginning to get a little light-headed, you know) expected the lieutenant to send in search of us, or wait till we returned. A likely thing for an officer in charge to do, with the lives of the sledging party depending on his getting them back to the ships, and only two men missing, who had broken orders and deserted their duty. A good riddance of bad rubbish -- that's what he said of us when we were reported missing, I'll be bound. When the light came we tried to get back; and we did set our course cleverly enough. But, bless you, we had nothing left to eat or drink! When the light failed us again we were done up. We dropped on the snow, under the lee of a rock, and gave out. The boatswain's mate said his prayers, and I said Amen. Not the least use! On the contrary, as the night advanced it got colder and colder. We were both close together, to keep each other warm. I don't know how long it was, I only know it was still pitch dark, when I heard the boatswain's mate give a little flutter of a sigh, and no more. I opened his clothes, and put my hand on his heart. Dead, of cold and exhaustion, and no mistake. I shouldn't have been long after him but for my own presence of mind.'

'Your presence of mind? What did you do?'

'Stripped every rag of clothes off him, and put them all on myself. What are you shivering about? He Couldn't feel it, could he? I tell you, he'd have been frozen stiff before the next day's light came -- but for my presence of mind again. As well as my failing strength would let me, I buried him under the snow. Virtue, they say, Master Alfred, is its own reward. That good action proved to be the saving of my life.'

'What do you mean?'

'Didn't I tell you I buried him?'

'Well!'

'Well, in that freezing air, the burying of him kept him eatable. Don't you see?'

'You wretch!'

'Put yourself in my place, and don't call names. I held out till I was mad with hunger. And then I did open my knife with my teeth. And I did burrow down in the snow till I felt him --.'

I could hear no more of it. 'Get on to the end! I said. 'Why didn't you die at the North Pole?'

'Because somebody helped me to get away.'

'Who helped you?'

'The Devil.'

He showed his yellow old teeth in a horrible grin. I could draw but one conclusion -- his mind was failing him before death. Anything that spared me his hideous confession of cannibalism was welcome. I asked how the supernatural rescue happened.

'More grog first,' he said. 'The horrors come on me when

I think of it.' He was evidently sinking. Without the grog I doubt if he could have said much more.

'I can't tell you how many days passed,' he went on; 'I only know that the time was nigh when it was all dark and no light. The darker it got, the deeper I scooped the sort of cavern I'd made for myself under the snow. Whether it was night, or whether it was day I know no more than you do. On a sudden, in the awful silence and solitude, I heard a voice, high up, as it were, on the rock behind me. It was a cheering and a pleasant voice, and it said, "Well, Septimus Notman, is there much left of the boatswain's mate by this time? Did he eat short while he lasted?" I cried out in fright, "Who the devil -- ?" The voice stopped me before I could say the rest. "You've hit it," says the voice, "I am that person; and it's about time the Devil helped you out of this." "No," says I, "I'd rather perish by cold than fire any day." "Make your mind easy," says he, taking the point, "I don't want you in my place yet. I expect you to do a deal more in the way of degrading your humanity before you come to me, and I offer you a safe passage back to the nearest settlement. Friend Septimus, you're a man after my own heart." "As how, sir?" says I. "Because you're such a complete beast," says he. "A human being who elevates himself, and rises higher and higher to his immortal destiny, is a creature I hate. He gets above me, even in his earthly lifetime. But you have dropped -- you dear good fellow -- to the level of a famished wolf. You have gobbled up your dead companion; and if you ever had such a thing as a soul -- ha, Septimus! -- it parted company with you at the first morsel you tasted of the Boatswain's mate. Do you think I'll leave such a prime specimen of the Animal Man as you are, deserted at the North Pole? No, no; I grant you a free pass by my railway; darkness and distance are no obstacles to Me. Are you ready?" You may not believe me; but I felt myself being lifted up, as it were, against my own will. "Give us a light," I says, "I can't travel in the dark." "Take my spectacles," says he, "they'll help you to see more than you bargain for. Look through them at your fellow mortals, and you'll see the inmost thoughts of their hearts as plain as I do, and, considering your nature, Septimus, that will drop you even below the level of a wolf." "Suppose I don't want to look," says I, "may I throw the spectacles away?" "They'll come back to you," says he. "May I smash them up?" "They'll put themselves together again." "What am I to do with them?" "Give them to another man. Now then! One, two, three -- and away!" You may not believe me again; I lost my senses, Master Alfred. Hold me up; I'm losing them now. More grog -- that's right -- more grog. I came to myself at Upernavik, with the Devil's Spectacles in my pocket. Take them, sir. And read those two ladies' hearts. And act accordingly. Hush! I hear him speaking to me again. Behind my pillow. Just as he spoke on the rock. Most polite and cheering. Calling to me, as it were, "Come, Cannibal -- come!" Like a song, isn't it? "Come, Cannibal -- come!"'

He sang the last words faintly, and died with a smile on his face. Delirium or lies? With the Spectacles actually in my hands, I was inclined to think lies. They were of the old-fashioned sort, with big, circular glasses, and stout tortoise-shell frames; they smelt musty, but not sulphurous. I possess a sense of humour, I am happy to say. When they were thoroughly cleaned, I determined to try the Devil's Spectacles on the two ladies, and submit to the consequences, whatever they might be."

II MEMOIRS OF MYSELF

Who were the two ladies?

They were both young and unmarried. As a matter of delicacy, I ask permission to mention them by their Christian names only. Zilla, aged seventeen. Cecilia, aged two and twenty.

And what was my position between them?

I was the same age as Cecilia. She was my mother's companion and reader; handsome, well-born and poor. I had made her a proposal, and had been accepted. There were no money difficulties in the way of our marriage, in spite of my sweetheart's empty purse. I was an only child, and I had inherited, excepting my mother's jointure, the whole of the large property that my father left at his death. In social rank Cecilia was more than my equal; we were therefore not ill-matched from the worldly point of view. Nevertheless, there was an obstacle to our union, and a person interested in making the most of it. The obstacle was Zilla. The person interested was my mother. Zilla was her niece -- her elder brother's daughter. The girl's parents had died in India, and she had been sent to school in England, under the care of her uncle and guardian. I had never seen her, and had hardly heard of her, until there was a question of her spending the Christmas holidays (in the year when Septimus Notman died) at our house.

'Her uncle has no objection,' my mother said; 'and I shall be more than glad to see her. A most interesting creature, as I hear. So lovely, and so good, that they call her Thenbsp;Angel, at school. I say nothing about her nice little fortune or the high military rank that her poor father possessed. You don't care for these things. But, oh, Alfred, it would make me so happy if you fell in love with Zilla and married her!'

Three days before, I had made my proposal to Cecilia, and had been accepted -- subject to my mother's approval. I thought this a good opportunity of stating my case plainly; and I spoke out. Never before had I seen my mother so outraged and disappointed -- enraged with Cecilia; disappointed with me. "A woman without a farthing of a dowry; a woman who was as old as I was; a woman who had taken advantage of her position in the house to mislead and delude me!' and so on. Cecilia would certainly have been sent away if I had not declared that I should feel it my duty, in that event, to marry her immediately. My mother knew my temper, and refrained from giving Cecilia any cause of offence. Cecilia, on her side, showed what is called a proper pride; she declined to become my wife until my mother approved of her. She considered herself to be a martyr; and I considered myself to be an abominably treated man. Between us, I am afraid we made our good mother's life unendurable -- she was obliged to be the first who gave way. It was understood that we were to be married in the spring. It was also understood that Zilla was bitterly disappointed at having her holiday visit to us put off. 'She was so anxious to see you, poor child,' my mother said to me; 'but I really daren't ask her here under present circumstances. She is so fresh, so innocent, so infinitely superior in personal attractions to Cecilia, that I don't know what might happen if you saw her now. You are the soul of honour, Alfred; but you and Zilla had better remain strangers to each other -- you might repent your rash engagement.' After this, it is needless to say that I was dying to see Zilla; while, at the same time, I never for an instant swerved from my fidelity to Cecilia.

Such was my position, on the memorable day when Septimus Notman died, leaving me possessor of the Devil's Spectacles.

III   THE TEST OF THE SPECTACLES

The first person whom I encountered on returning to the house was the butler. He met me in the hall, with a receipted account in his hand which I had sent him to pay. The amount was close on a hundred pounds, and I had paid it immediately. 'Is there no discount?' I asked, looking at the receipt.

'The parties expect cash, sir, and charge accordingly.'

He looked so respectable when he made this answer, he had served us for so many years, that I felt an irresistible temptation to try the Devil's Spectacles on the butler, before I ventured to look through them at the ladies of my family. Our honest old servant would be such an excellent test.

'I am afraid my sight is failing me,' I said.

With this exceedingly simple explanation I put on the spectacles and looked at the butler.

The hall whirled round with me; on my word of honour I tremble and turn cold while I write of it now. Septimus Notman had spoken the truth!

In an instant the butler's heart became hideously visible -- a fat organ seen through the medium of the infernal glasses. The thought in him was plainly legible to me in these words: 'Does my master think I'm going to give him the five per cent off the bill? Beastly meanness, interfering with the butler's perquisites.'

I took off my spectacles and put them in my pocket.

'You are a thief,' I said to the butler. 'You have got the discount money on this bill -- five pounds all but a shilling or two -- in your pocket. Send in your accounts; you leave my service.'

'To-morrow, sir, if you like!' answered the butler, indignantly. 'After serving your family for five-and-twenty years, to be called a thief for only taking my perquisites is an insult, Mr Alfred, that I have not deserved.' He put his handkerchief to his eyes and left me.

It was true that he had served us for a quarter of a century; it was also true that he had taken his perquisite and told a fib about it. But he had his compensating virtues. When I was a child he had given me many a ride on his knee and many a stolen drink of wine and water. His cellar-book had always been honestly kept; and his wife herself admitted that he was a model husband. At other times I should have remembered this, I should have felt that I had been hasty, and have asked his pardon. At this time I failed to feel the slightest compassion for him, and never faltered for a moment in my resolution to send him away. What change had passed over me?

The library door opened, and an old schoolfellow and college friend of mine looked out. 'I thought I heard your voice in the hall,' he said; 'I have been waiting an hour for you.'

'Anything very important,' I asked, leading the way back to the library.

'Nothing of the least importance to you,' he replied, modestly.

I wanted no further explanation. More than once already

I had lent him money, and, sooner or later, he had always repaid me. 'Another little loan?' I inquired, smiling pleasantly.

'I am really ashamed to ask you again, Alfred. But if you could lend me fifty pounds -- just look at that letter?'

He made some joke, suggested by the quaint appearance of the Spectacles. I was too closely occupied to appreciate his sense of humour. What had he just said to me? He had said. 'I am ashamed to ask you again.' And what had he thought while he was speaking? He had thought. 'When one has a milch cow at one's disposal, who but a fool would fail to take advantage of it?'

I handed him back the letter (from a lawyer, threatening 'proceedings') and I said, in my hardest tones, 'It's not convenient to oblige you this time.'

He stared at me like a man thunderstruck. 'Is this a joke, Alfred?' he asked.

'Do I look as if I was joking?'

He took up his hat. 'There is but one excuse for you,' he said. 'Your social position is too much for your weak brain -- your money has got into your head. Good morning.'

I had been indebted to him for all sorts of kind services at school and college. He was an honourable man, and a faithful friend. If the galling sense of his own narrow means made him unjustly contemptuous towards rich people, it was a fault (in my case, an exasperating fault), no doubt. But who is perfect? And what are fifty pounds to me? This is what I should once have felt, before he could have found time enough to get to the door. As things were, I let him go, and thought myself well rid of a mean hanger-on who only valued me for my money.

Being now free to visit the ladies, I rang the bell and asked if my mother was at home. She was in her boudoir. And where was Miss Cecilia? In the boudoir, too.

On entering the room I found visitors in the way, and put off the trial of the Spectacles until they had taken their leave. Just as they were going a thundering knock at the door announced more visitors. This time, fortunately, we escaped with no worse consequences than the delivery of cards. We actually had two minutes to ourselves. I seized the opportunity of reminding my mother that I was constitutionally inaccessible to the claims of Society, and that I thought we might as well have our house to ourselves for half an hour or so. 'Send word down stairs,' I said, 'that you are not at home.'

My mother -- magnificent in her old lace, her admirably-dressed grey hair, and her finely falling robe of purple-silk -- looked across the fireplace at Cecilia -- tall, and lazy, and beautiful, with lovely brown eyes, luxuriant black hair, a warmly-pale complexion, and an amber-coloured dress -- and said to me, 'You forget Cecilia. She likes Society.'

Cecilia looked at my mother with an air of languid surprise. 'What an extraordinary mistake! she answered. 'I hate Society.'

My mother smiled -- rang the bell -- and gave the order -- Not at home. I produced my spectacles. There was an outcry at the hideous ugliness of them. I laid blame on 'my oculist,' and waited for what was to follow between the two ladies. My mother spoke. Consequently I looked at my mother.

[I present her words first, and her thoughts next, in parenthesis.]

'So you hate society, my dear? Surely you have changed your opinion lately?' ('She doesn't mind how she lies as long as she can curry favour with Alfred. False creature.')

[I report Cecilia's answer on the same plan.]

'Pardon me; I haven't in the least changed my opinion -- I was only afraid to express it. I hope I have not given offence by expressing it now.' ('She can't exist without gossip, and then she tries to lay it on me. Worldly old wretch!')

What I began to think of my mother, I am ashamed to record. What I thought of Cecilia may be stated in two words. I was more eager than ever to see 'The Angel of the school,' the good and lovely Zilla.

My mother stopped the further progress of my investigations. 'Take off those hideous Spectacles, Alfred, or leave us to our visitors. I don't say your sight may not be failing; I only say change your oculist.'

I took off the Spectacles, all the more willingly that I began to be really afraid of them. The talk between the ladies went on.

'Yours is a strange confession, my dear,' my mother said to Cecilia. 'May I ask what motive so young a lady can have for hating Society?'

'Only the motive of wanting to improve myself,' Cecilia

answered. 'If I knew a little more of modern languages, and if I could be something better than a feeble amateur when I paint in water colours, you might think me worthier to be Alfred's wife. But Society is always in the way when I open my book or take up my brushes. In London I have no time to myself, and, I really can't disguise it, the frivolous life I lead is not to my taste.'

I thought this -- (my Spectacles being in my pocket, remember) -- very well and very prettily said. My mother looked at me. 'I quite agree with Cecilia,' I said, answering the look. 'We cannot count on having five minutes to ourselves in London from morning to night.' Another knock at the street door contributed its noisy support to my views as I spoke. 'We daren't even look out of the window,' I remarked, 'for fear Society may look up at the same moment, and see that we are at home.'

My mother smiled. 'You are certainly two remarkable young people,' she said, with an air of satirical indulgence -- and paused for a moment, as if an idea had occurred to her which was more than usually worthy of consideration. If her eye had not been on me at the moment, I believe I should have taken my Spectacles out of my pocket. 'You are both so thoroughly agreed in disliking Society and despising London,' she resumed, 'that I feel it my duty, as a good mother, to make your lives a little more in harmony with your tastes, if I can. You complain, Alfred, that you can never count on having five minutes to yourself with Cecilia, Cecilia complains that she is perpetually interrupted in the laudable effort to improve her mind. I offer you both the whole day to yourselves, week after week, for the next three months. We will spend the winter at Long Fallas.'

Long Fallas was our country seat. There was no hunting; the shooting was let; the place was seven miles from Timbercombe town and station; and our nearest neighbour was a young Ritualistic clergyman, popularly reported in the village to be starving himself to death. I declined my mother's extraordinary proposal without a moment's hesitation. Cecilia, with the readiest and sweetest submission, accepted it.

This was our first open difference of opinion. Even without the Spectacles I could see that my mother hailed it as a good sign. She had consented to our marriage in the spring, without in the least altering her opinion that the angelic Zilla was the right wife for me. 'Settle it between yourselves, my dears,' she said, and left her chair to look for her work. Cecilia rose immediately to save her the trouble.

The instant their backs were turned on me I put on the terrible glasses. Is there such a thing in anatomy as a back view of the heart? There is such a thing assuredly when you look through the Devil's Spectacles. My mother's private sentiments presented themselves to me, as follows: 'If they don't get thoroughly sick of each other in a winter at Long Fallas I give up all knowledge of human nature. He shall marry Zilla yet.' Cecilia's motives asserted themselves with transparent simplicity in these words, 'His mother fully expects me to say "No." Horrible as the prospect is, I'll disappoint her by saying "Yes."'

'Horrible as the prospect is' was to my mind a very revolting expression, considering that I was personally included in the prospect. My mother's mischievous test of our affection for each other now presented itself to me in the light of a sensible proceeding. In the solitude of Long Fallas, I should surely discover whether Cecilia was about to marry me for my money or for myself. I concealed my Spectacles, and said nothing at the time. But later, when my mother entered the drawing-room dressed to go out for dinner, I waylaid her, quite willing to go to Long Fallas. Cecilia came in dressed for dinner also. She had never looked so irresistibly lovely as when she was informed of my change of opinion. 'What a happy time we shall have,' she said, and smiled as if she really meant it?

They went away to their party. I was in the library when they returned. Hearing the carriage stop at the door I went out into the hall, and was suddenly checked on my way to the ladies by the sound of a man's voice: 'Many thanks; I am close at home now.' My mother's voice followed: 'I will let you know if we go to the country, Sir John. You will ride over and see us?' 'With thee greatest pleasure. Good-night, Miss Cecilia.' There was no mistaking the tone in which those last four words were spoken. Sir John's accent expressed indescribable tenderness. I retired again to the library.

My mother came in, followed by her charming companion.

'Here is a new complication,' she said. 'Cecilia doesn't

want to go to Long Fallas.' I asked why. Cecilia answered, without looking at me, 'Oh, I have changed my mind. She turned aside to relieve my mother of her fur cloak. I instantly consulted my Spectacles, and obtained my information in these mysterious terms: 'Sir John goes to Timbercombe.'

Very short, and yet suggestive of more than one interpretation. A little inquiry made the facts more clear. Sir John had been one of the guests at the dinner, and he and Cecilia had shaken hands like old friends. At my mother's request, he had been presented to her. He had produced such an excellent impression that she had taken him in her carriage part of his way home. She had also discovered that he was about to visit a relative living at Timbercombe (already mentioned, I think, as our nearest town). Another momentary opportunity with the Spectacles completed my discoveries. Sir John had proposed marriage (unsuccessfully) to Cecilia, and being still persistently in love with her, only wanted a favourable opportunity to propose again. The excellent impression which he had produced on my mother was perfectly intelligible now.

In feeling reluctant to give her rejected lover that other opportunity, was Cecilia afraid of Sir John, or afraid of herself? My Spectacles informed me that she deliberately declined to face that question, even in her thoughts.

Under these circumstances, the test of a dreary winter residence at Long Fallas became, to my mind, more valuable than ever. Single-handed, Cecilia might successfully keep up appearances and deceive other people, though she might not deceive me. But, in combination with Sir John, there was a chance that she might openly betray the true state of her feelings. If I was really the favoured man, she would, of course, be dearer to me than ever. If not (with more producible proof than the Devil's Spectacles to justify me), I need not hesitate to break off the engagement.

'Second thoughts are not always best, dear Cecilia,' I said. 'Do me a favour. Let us try Long Fallas, and if we find the place quite unendurable, let us return to London.'

Cecilia looked at me and hesitated -- looked at my mother, and submitted to Long Fallas in the sweetest manner. The more they were secretly at variance, the better the two ladies appeared to understand each other.

We did not start for the country until three days afterward. The packing up was a serious matter to begin with, and my mother prolonged the delay by paying a visit to her niece at the school in the country. She kept the visit a secret from Cecilia, of course. But even when we were alone, and when I asked about Zilla, I was only favoured with a very brief reply. She merely lifted her eyes to Heaven, and said, 'Perfectly charming!'

IV THE TEST OF LONG FALLAS

We had had a week of it. If we had told each other the truth we should have said, 'Let us go back to London.'

Thus far there had been no signs of Sir John. The Spectacles informed me that he had arrived at Timbercombe, and that Cecilia had written to him. But, strangely enough, they failed to disclose what she had said. Has she forgotten it already, or was there some defect, hitherto unsuspected, in my supernatural glasses?

Christmas Day was near at hand. The weather was, so far, almost invariably misty and wet. Cecilia began to yawn over her favourite intellectual resources. My mother waited with superhuman patience for events. As for myself, having literally nothing else to amuse me, I took to gratifying an improper curiosity in the outlying regions of the family circle. In plain English, I discovered a nice little needle-woman, who was employed at Long Fallas. Her name was Miss Peskey. When nobody was looking, I amused myself with Miss Peskey.

Let no person of strict principles be alarmed. It was an innocent flirtation, on my side; and the nice little needle-woman rigidly refused to give me the smallest encouragement. Quite a young girl, Miss Peskey had the self-possession of a mature woman. She allowed me time to see that she had a trim little figure, soft blue eyes, and glossy golden hair; and then, in the sweetest of voices, respectfully requested me to leave her to her work. If I tried to persuade her to let me stay a little longer, she rose meekly, and said 'I shall, most unwillingly, be compelled to place myself under the protection of the housekeeper.' Once I attempted to take her hand. She put her handkerchief to her eyes and said, 'Is it manly, sir, to insult a defenceless girl?' In one word, Miss Peskey foiled me at every point. For the first week I never even got the chance of looking at her through the Devil's Spectacles.

On the first day of the new week the weather cleared up wonderfully; spring seemed to have come to us in the middle of winter.

Cecilia and I went out riding. On our return, having nothing better to do, I accompanied the horses back to the stables, and naturally offended the groom, who thought I was 'watching him.' Returning toward the house, I passed the window of the ground-floor room, at the back of the building, devoted to the needlewoman. A railed yard kept me at a respectful distance, but at the same time gave me a view of the interior of the room. Miss Peskey was not alone; my mother was with her. They were evidently talking, but not a word reached my ears. It mattered nothing. While I could see them through my Spectacles, their thoughts were visible to me before they found their way into words.

My mother was speaking -- 'Well, my dear, have you formed your opinion of him yet?'

Miss Peskey replied, 'Not quite yet.'

'You are wonderfully cautious in arriving at a conclusion. How much longer is this clever contrivance of yours to last?'

'Give me two days more, dear madam; I can't decide until

Sir John helps me.'

'Is Sir John really coming here?'

'I think so.'

'And have you managed it?'

'If you will kindly excuse me, I would rather not answer just yet.'

The housekeeper entered the room, and called my mother away on some domestic business. As she walked to the door, I had time to read her thought before she went out -- 'Very extraordinary to find such resources of clever invention in such a young girl!'

Miss Peskey, left in maiden meditation with her work on her lap, smiled to herself. I turned the glasses on her, and made a discovery that petrified me. To put it plainly, the charming needlewoman was deceiving us all (with the one exception of my mother) under an assumed name and vocation in life. Miss Peskey was no other than my cousin Zilla, 'the Angel of the school!'

Let me do my poor mother justice. She was guilty of the consenting to the deception, and of no more. The invention of the trick, and the entire responsibility of carrying it out, rested wholly and exclusively with Miss Zilla, aged seventeen.

I followed the train of thought which my mother's questions had set going in the mind of this young person. To justify my own conduct, I must report the result as briefly as I can. Have you heard of 'fasting' girls? have you heard of 'mesmeric' girls? have you heard of girls (in the newspapers) who have invented the most infamous charges against innocent men? Then don't accuse my Spectacles of seeing impossible sights!

My report of Miss Zilla's thoughts, as they succeeded each other, begins as follows:

First Thought: 'My small fortune is all very well; but I want to be mistress of a great establishment, and get away from school. Alfred, dear fellow, is reported to have fifteen thousand a year. Is his mother's companion to be allowed to catch this rich fish, without the least opposition? Not if I know it!'

Second Thought: 'How very simple old people are! His mother visits me, invites me to Long Fallas, and expects me to cut out Cecilia. Men are such fools (the writing master has fallen in love with me) that she would only have to burst out crying, and keep him to herself. I have proposed a better way than fair fighting for Alfred, suggested by a play I read the other day. The old mother consents, with conditions. "I am sure you will do nothing, my dear, unbecoming to a young lady. Win him, as Miss Hardcastle won Mr Marlow in She Stoops to Conquer, if you like; but do nothing to forfeit your self-respect." What astonishing simplicity! Where did she go to school when she was young?'

Third Thought: 'How amazingly lucky that Cecilia's maid is lazy, and that the needlewoman dines in the servants' hall! The maid had the prospect of getting up before six in the morning, to be ready to go in the chaise-car with the servant who does the household errands at Timbercombe -- and for what? To take a note from her mistress to Sir John, and wait for an answer. The good little needlewoman hears this, smiles, and says, "I don't mind how early I get up; I'll take it for you, and bring back the answer."'

Fourth Thought: 'What a blessing it is to have blue eyes and golden hair! Sir John was quite struck with me. I thought at the time he would do instead of Alfred. Fortunately I have since asked the simple old mother about him. He is a poor baronet. Not to be thought of for an instant. "My Lady" -- without a corresponding establishment! Too dreadful! But I didn't throw away my fascinations. I saw him wince when he read the letter. "No bad news, I hope, sir," I ventured to say. He shook his head solemnly. "Your mistress" (he took me, of course, for Cecilia's maid) forbids me to call at Long Fallas." I thought to myself what a hypocrite Cecilia must be, and I said modestly to Sir John, to keep up appearances. Our private arrangement is that he is to ride over to Long Fallas to-morrow, and wait in the shrubbery at half-past two. If it rains or snows he is to try the next fine day. In either case the poor needlewoman will ask for a half holiday, and will induce Miss Cecilia to take a little walk in the right direction. Sir John gave me two sovereigns and a kiss at parting. I accepted both tributes with the most becoming humility. He shall have his money's worth, though he is a poor baronet; he shall meet his young lady in the shrubbery. And I may catch the rich fish, after all!'

Fifth Thought: 'Bother this horrid work! It is all very well to be clever with one's needle, but how it disfigures one's forefinger! No matter, I must play my part while it lasts, or I shall be reported lazy by the most detestable woman I ever met with -- the housekeeper at Long Fallas.'

She threaded her needle, and I put my Spectacles in my pocket.

I don't think I suspected it at the time; but I am now well aware that Septimus Notman's diabolical gift was exerting an influence over me. I was wickedly cool, under circumstances which would have roused my righteous indignation in the days before my Spectacles. Sir John and the Angel; my mother and her family interests; Cecilia and her unacknowledged lover -- what a network of conspiracy and deception was wound about me! and what a perfectly fiendish pleasure I felt in planning to match them on their own ground! The method of obtaining this object presented itself to me in the simplest form. I had only to take my mother for a walk in the near neighbourhood of the shrubbery -- and the exposure would be complete! That night I studied the barometer with unutterable anxiety. The prospect of the weather was all that I could wish.

V THE TRUTH IN THE SHRUBBERY

On the next day, the friendly sun shone, the balmy air invited everybody to go out. I made no further use of the Spectacles that morning: my purpose was to keep them in my pocket until the interview in the shrubbery was over. Shall I own the motive? It was simply fear -- fear of making further discoveries, and of losing the masterly self-control on which the whole success of my project depended.

We lunched at one o'clock. Had Cecilia and Zilla come to a private understanding on the subject of the interview in the shrubbery? By way of ascertaining this, I asked Cecilia if she would like to go out riding in the afternoon. She declined the proposal -- she wanted to finish a sketch. I was sufficiently answered.

'Cecilia complains that your manner has grown cold toward her lately,' mother said, when we were left together.

My mind was dwelling on Cecilia's letter to Sir John. Would any man have so easily adopted Zilla's suggestion not to take Cecilia on her word, unless there had been something to encourage him? I could only trust myself to answer my mother very briefly. 'Cecilia is changed towards me' -- was all my reply.

My mother was evidently gratified by this prospect of a misunderstanding between us. 'Ah!' she said, 'if Cecilia only had Zilla's sweet temper.'

This was a little too much to endure -- but I did endure it. 'Will you come out with me, mamma, for a walk in the grounds?' I asked.

My mother accepted the invitation so gladly, that I really think I should have felt ashamed of myself -- if I had not had the contaminating Spectacles in my pocket. We had just settled to start soon after two o'clock, when there was a timid knock at the door. The angelic needlewoman appeared to ask for her half holiday. My mother actually blushed! Old habits will cling to the members of the past generation. 'What is it?' she said, in low uncertain tones. 'Might I go to the village, ma'am, to buy some little things?' 'Certainly.' The door closed again. 'Now for the shrubbery!' I thought. 'Make haste, mamma,' I said, 'the best of the day is going. And mind one thing -- put on your thickest boots!'

On one side of the shrubbery were the gardens. The other side was bounded by a wooden fence. A footpath, running part of the way beside the fence, crossed the grass beyond, and made a short cut between the nearest park gate and the servants' offices. This was the safe place that I had chosen. We could hear perfectly -- though the closely-planted evergreens might prevent the exercise of sight. I had recommended 'thick boots' because there was no help but to muffle the sound of our footsteps by walking on the wet grass. At its further end, the shrubbery joined the carriage road up to the house.

My mother's surprise at the place that I had chosen for our walk would have been expressed in words, as well as by looks, if I had not stopped her by a whispered warning. 'Keep perfectly quiet,' I said, "and listen. I have a motive for bringing you here.'

The words had hardly passed my lips, before we heard the voices of Cecilia and the needlewoman in the shrubbery.

'Wait a minute,' said Cecilia; 'you must be a little more explicit, before I consent to go any farther. How came you to take my letter to Sir John, instead of my maid?'

'Only to oblige her, Miss. She was not very well, and she didn't fancy going all the way to Timbercombe. I can buy no good needles in the village, and I was glad of the opportunity of getting to the town.'

There was a pause. Cecilia was reflecting, as I supposed. My mother began to turn pale.

Cecilia resumed. 'There is nothing in Sir John's answer to my letter,' she said, ' that leads me to suppose he can be guilty of an act of rudeness. I have always believed him to be a gentleman. No gentleman would force his way into my presence, when I wrote expressly to ask him to spare me. Pray how did you know he was determined only to take his dismissal from my lips?'

'Gentlemen's feelings sometimes get the better of them, Miss. Sir John was very much distressed --'

Cecilia interrupted her. 'There was nothing in my letter to distress him,' she said.

'He was distressed, Miss; and he did say, "I cannot take my answer this way -- I must and will see her." And then he asked me to get you to walk out to-day, and to say nothing so that he might take you by surprise. He is so madly in love with you, Miss, that he is all but beside himself. I am really afraid of what might happen, if you don't soften his disappointment to him in some way. How any lady can treat such a handsome gentleman so cruelly, passes my poor judgement!'

Cecilia instantly resented the familiarity implied in those last words. 'You are not called upon to exercise your judgement,' she said. 'You can go back to the house.'

'Hadn't I better see Sir John first, Miss?'

'Certainly not! You and Sir John have seen quite enough of each other already.'

There was another pause. My mother stood holding by my arm, pale and trembling. We could neither of us speak. My own mind was strangely agitated. Either Cecilia was a monster of deceit, or she had thus far spoken and acted as became a true and highly-bred woman. The distant sound of horses' hoofs on the park road, told us both that the critical moment was at hand. In another minute, the sound ceased. Sir John had probably dismounted, and tied up his horse at the entrance of the shrubbery. After an interval, we heard Cecilia's voice again, farther away from us. We followed the voice. The interview which was to decide my future destiny in life had begun.

'No, Sir John; I must have my question answered first. Is there anything in my letter -- was there anything in my conduct, when we met in London -- which justifies this?'

'Love justifies everything, Cecilia!'

'You are not to call me Cecilia, if you please. Have you no plainer answer to give me?'

41

'Have you no mercy on a man, who cannot live without you? Is there really nothing in myself and my title to set against the perfectly obscure person, to whom you have so rashly engaged yourself? It would be an insult to suppose that his wealth has tempted you. What can be his merit in your eyes? His own friends can say no more in his favour than that he is a good-natured fool. I don't blame you; women often drift into engagements that they repent of afterwards. Do yourself justice! Be true to the nobility of character -- and be the angel who makes our two lives happy, before it is too late!'

'Have you done, Sir John?'

There was a moment of silence. It was impossible to mistake her tone -- Sir John's flow of eloquence came to a full stop.

'Before I answer you,' Cecilia proceeded, 'I have something to say first. The girl who took my letter to you, was not my maid, as you may have supposed. She is a stranger to me; and I suspect her of being a false creature with some purpose of her own to serve. I find a difficulty in attributing to a person in your rank of life the mean deceit which answers my letter in terms that lead me to trust you, and then takes me by surprise in this way. My messenger (as I believe) is quite insolent enough to have suggested this course to you. Am I right? I expect a reply, Sir John, that is worthy in its entire truthfulness of you and your title. Am I right?'

'You are right, Miss Cecilia. Pray don't despise me. The temptation to plead with you once more --'

'I will speak to you, Sir John, as candidly as you have

spoken to me. You are entirely wrong in supposing it possible for me to repent of my marriage engagement. The man, whose false friends have depreciated him in your estimation, is the only man I love, and the only man I will marry. And I beg you to understand, if he lost the whole of his fortune to-morrow, I would marry him the next day, if he asked me. Must I say more? or will you treat me with the delicacy of a gentleman, and take your leave?'

I don't remember whether he said anything or not, before he left her. I only know that they parted. Don't ask me to confess what I felt. Don't ask me to describe what my mother felt. Let the scene be changed, and the narrative be resumed at a later hour of the day.

VI   THE END OF THE SPECTACLES

I asked myself a question, which I beg to repeat here. What did I owe to the Devil's Spectacles?

In the first place, I was indebted to my glasses for seeing all the faults, and none of the merits, in the persons about me. In the second place, I arrived at the discovery that, if we are to live usefully and happily with our fellow-creatures, we must take them at their best, and not at their worst. Having reached these conclusions, I trusted my own unassisted insight, and set myself to ascertain what the Devil had not helped me to discover in the two persons who were dearest to me -- my mother and Cecilia.

I began with Cecilia, leaving my mother time to recover after the shock that had fallen on her.

It was impossible to acknowledge what I had seen through the Spectacles, or what I had heard at the shrubbery fence. In speaking to Cecilia, I could only attribute my coldness of manner to jealousy of the mere name of 'Sir John,' and ask to be pardoned for even a momentary distrust of the most constant and charming of women. There was something, I suppose, in my contrite consciousness of having wronged her, that expressed itself in my looks and in my tones. We were sitting together on the sofa. For the first time since our engagement, she put her arm around my neck, and kissed me, without waiting to be kissed first.

I am not very demonstrative,' she said, softly; 'and I don't think, Alfred, you have ever known how fond I am of you.

44

My dear, when Sir John and I met again at that dinner party, I was too faithful to you to even allow myself to think of him. Your poor mother irritated me by seeming to doubt whether I could trust myself within reach of Timbercombe, or I should never have consented to go to Long Fallas. You remember that she invited Sir John to ride over and see us. I wrote to him, informing him of my engagement to you, and telling him, in the plainest words, that if he did call at this house, nothing would induce me to see him. I had every reason to suppose that he would understand and respect my motives --'

She paused. The rich colour rose in her lovely face. I refused to let her distress herself by saying a word of what had happened in the shrubbery. Look back, if you have forgotten it, and see how completely the Spectacles failed to show me the higher and nobler motives that had animated her. The little superficial irritabilities and distrusts, they exhibited to perfection; but the true regard for each other, hidden below the surface in my mother and in my promised wife, was completely beyond them.

'Shall we go back to London, to-morrow?' I asked.

'Are you tired of being here with me, Alfred?'

'I am tired of waiting till the spring, my angel. I will live with you wherever you like, if you will only consent to hasten the transformation which makes you my wife. Will you consent?'

'If your mother asks me. Don't hurry her, Alfred.'

But I did hurry her. After what we had heard in the

shrubbery I could look into my mother's heart (without assistance), and feel sure that the nobler part of her nature would justify my confidence in it. She was not only ready to 'ask Cecilia,' then and there -- she was eager, poor soul, to confess hoe completely she had been mislaid by her natural interest in her brother's child. Being firmly resolved to keep the secret of my discovery of her niece, I refused to hear her, as I had refused to hear Cecilia. Did I not know, without being told, what child's play it would be to Zilla to dazzle and delude my innocent mother? I merely asked if 'the needlewoman was still in the house.' The answer was thoroughly explicit: 'She is at the railway station by this time, and she will never enter any house of mine again.'

We returned to London the next morning.

I had a moment's private talk with the station-master at Timbercombe. Sir John had left his friends at the town, on the previous day. He and Zilla had met on the platform, waiting for the London train. She had followed him into the smoking-carriage. Just as the station-master was going to start the train, Sir John opened the door, with a strong expression of disgust, and took refuge in another carriage. She had tried the baronet as a last resource, and he had slipped through her fingers too. What did it matter to Zilla? She had plenty of time before her, and she belonged to the order of persons who never fail to make the most of her advantages. The other day I saw the announcement of her marriage to a great ironmaster, a man worth millions of money, with establishments to correspond. Bravo, Zilla! No need to look for your nobler motives with the naked eye.

A few days before I became a married man I was a guest at the dinner table of a bachelor friend, and I met Sir John. It would have been ridiculous to leave the room; I merely charged my host to keep my name concealed. I sat next to the baronet, and he doesn't know, to this day, who his 'very agreeable neighbour' was.

Instead of spending our honeymoon abroad, Cecilia and I went back to Long Fallas. We found the place delightful, even in the winter time.

Did I take the Devil's Spectacles back with me?

No.

Did I throw them away or smash them into small morsels?

Neither. I remembered what Septimus Notman had told me. The one way of getting rid of them was to give them to some other man.

And to what other man did I give them?

I had not forgotten what my rival had said of me in the shrubbery. I gave the Devil's Spectacles to Sir John.

VII. BETWEEN THE READER AND THE EDITOR

Are we to have no satisfactory explanation of the supernatural element in the story? How did it come into the Editor's hands? Was there neither name or address on the manuscript?

There was an address, if you must know. But I decline to mention it.

Suppose I guess that the address was at a lunatic asylum? What would you say to that?

I should say I suspected you of being a critic, and I should have the honour of wishing you good morning.